ADDING UP TO MURDER

DOG DETECTIVE - THE BEAGLE MYSTERIES BOOK 8

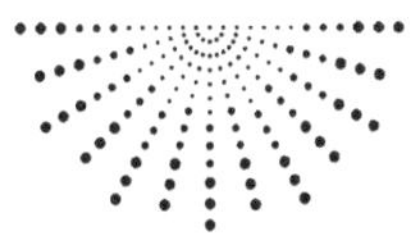

ROSIE SAMS

AGATHA PARKER

SWEETBOOKHUB.COM

THE DOG DETECTIVE – THE BEAGLE MYSTERIES

Welcome to my new book. I joined forces with the amazing Rosie Sams to work on this wonderful series of cozy mystery books all featuring a sweet little Beagle puppy. Mazie is an ex-police dog who was wounded in service. She is gifted to Hannah Barry, a broken-hearted realtor who is down on her luck.

At first, Hannah is unsure, can she learn to love the Beagle? What will she do when a body is found?

If you missed it, find out how Mazie found a new home, and Hannah some peace, in book one of this series Sniffing out the killer each book can be read alone.

Rosie has a free book Smudge and the Stolen Puppies that you can pick up. It is about an amazing and cute French Bulldog the best Dog Detective in all of Port Warren. Grab it here for FREE

"Are you hungry, Mazie?" Hannah clipped the tricolored beagle's leash onto her collar as her dog's tail wagged back and forth. Mazie was always hungry and always ready for a walk. Stepping out the door, the two of them made their way into the springtime air of Blairstown, Vermont.

Hannah breathed in the fresh air, appreciating the tiny flower buds pushing through the earth, attempting to make their return to the small town's pretty landscaping.

Hannah and Mazie were heading to Troughton's Trough. The owner of the fine dining establishment, Colin Troughton, was waiting there with a special table for them. It had become their routine to meet

Colin, Hannah's boyfriend, there for lunch during the lull between the lunch and dinner rushes. Mazie trotted along the sidewalk happily, almost pulling Hannah with her for she knew exactly where they were headed.

Mazie waited at the door for Hannah to open it, and as she did, they were greeted with the sweet scent of chocolate cake baking in the oven. "Hmm. That smells amazing!" Hannah said. "Does that mean Molten Lava Cake is the dessert special for tonight?"

Colin looked up from a seat at a table in the corner. "Hannah! Mazie!" He stood to greet his girlfriend, giving Hannah a quick kiss on the cheek before he leaned over to scratch Mazie behind her ears. "Come on over, lunch is ready." They followed him to their regular table when Hannah noticed someone sitting in the shadows from the table Colin guided her to.

"Oh! I'm sorry to interrupt, I didn't realize you had another guest," Hannah said.

The man stood abruptly. "Hello there, my name is Frederick Hogan. I'm Colin's accountant." The man was tall but stooped with scruffy brown hair that was a little too long. Dark framed and large glasses covered his blue eyes, which didn't meet hers as he extended his hand to Hannah.

She reached to shake it and was surprised at his loose grip.

His eyes darted to the floor and he backed up, tripping over his chair. "Oh, whoops." He pushed his glasses up the bridge of his nose shyly, still unable to meet Hannah's eyes.

Hannah couldn't help but feel bad for the self-conscious man. She took in his dark hair and his blue eyes and thought he could be attractive... if he had just a bit more confidence.

"Oh!" Frederick said suddenly when his glance caught on Mazie. "Is that a beagle? I love beagles!" He took a piece of chicken from his plate and tossed it to Mazie. Then his eyes shot up to Hannah. "Was that okay to do?"

Hannah smiled. "More than okay. Mazie will love you forever."

The shy man grinned. "The feeling will be mutual, then!"

Mazie quickly became comfortable with Frederick,

to the point where she'd climbed up on his lap and was sitting on it as though she were a baby soaking up the cuddles. Fredrick seemed much more relaxed and was stroking and cooing to her.

Hannah and Colin looked on in amusement. "She looks like a human," Hannah said. "She loves you!"

A blush crept up Frederick's neck and he patted Mazie's head, feeding the beagle until all the remains of his chicken was gone from his plate. Moving it to the side, he slid the accounting papers in front of him. "So, Colin - any questions about your finances?"

Though Mazie was finished eating, she wasn't finished sniffing. She took a keen interest in Frederick's paper. She was so interested; she began licking the paper.

"Mazie! Leave it," Hannah said. "I don't want you to get ink poisoning."

Frederick moved the papers away from the dog and put her on the floor.

"That's so strange, I've never seen her do that before," Hannah said.

Frederick shrugged. "Maybe it's the ink. I use a

special type that is made for me by a friend. She will be fine; it's organic and vegan certified, but I've never seen a dog react this way."

"It's no problem, Frederick. Vegan, weren't you eating chicken?"

"Oh, yes, my friend is a vegan and she's trying to make a business out of artisan ink."

"How nice." Hannah nodded to the breadbasket. "Feel free to give her as much of that as you'd like, though!"

So, Frederick did. He laughed and tossed piece after piece of the fresh bread to Mazie, the dog nuzzling closer and closer to him with each bite he tossed. "It would break my heart if the ink from my pen caused this little cutie any harm."

At this, Mazie sat in front of him and gave a little woof, causing everyone at the table to laugh.

When his plate was fully empty, Fredrick turned to Colin. "I'll leave you two to catch up. Just remember, Colin. With those few easy changes I mentioned, you can really save some money around here." He stood up, and reluctantly leaving Mazie, he leaned down to kiss her on the head.

"Thanks, Frederick!" Colin called after him as he left the restaurant.

When he was safely out on the street, Hannah turned to Colin, her eyes sparkling.

"Nope," he shook his head. "Don't even think about it."

Hannah grinned from ear to ear. "Frederick seems sweet, is he single?"

Colin groaned. "I said not to think about it!" he said. "We are not going to set him up with anyone."

Hannah pretended not to hear him. "He's so sweet. Maybe a little awkward, but don't you think he deserves to be happy?" she asked.

Colin put his hand on her arm. "Hannah, I think he's plenty happy. He doesn't need to be dating to be happy."

Hannah nodded. "Yes. No, of course not. He's just so kind. You could tell by the way he treated Mazie. It's a real pity that he seems so lonely."

"I agree with you that he's a very kind man. He's also excellent at his job. His business is doing so well, I doubt he has much time to think about love," he said. "In fact, he's on his way right now to take a meeting with Lucas Blake."

Hannah cocked her head. "Who?"

"He's a wealthy art dealer in town who is evidently planning to reinvest most of his significant assets." Colin raised an eyebrow at Hannah. "People like him only work with the very best."

Hannah thought about what Colin said while she took a few bites of her pasta. "I'm sure he's amazing, but I still think that Frederick is worthy of more than just another client."

Mazie, who'd been sitting under the table, yapped her approval at Hannah's statement, causing Hannah and Colin to laugh.

CHAPTER TWO

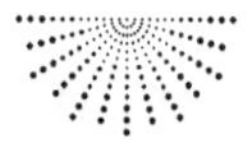

$\mathcal{A}$ few days later, Hannah was enjoying a cup of coffee at her favorite shop: Jolt of Java. Her good friends, Oscar and Anita Gomez, owned the quaint shop which was popular among the locals. When it was time for their break, they joined her at her table.

"Do you have any new cases, anything interesting or juicy?" Oscar asked with a wink. When she'd started off on her journey to become a Private Investigator, Oscar and Anita were none too supportive, that is, until she managed to put her detective skills to use vindicating Oscar from being falsely accused of a murder. Since then, they'd been her biggest supporters. They even shadowed her on her most recent case, making them much more invested in her work.

"Stop looking for gossip," Anita said slapping her husband's arm playfully.

"I'm not, more for excitement."

Anita slapped him again. The couple were both attractive, both committed to their coffee shop, their olive-skinned good looks were always accompanied by a smile and their love for each other shone through.

Hannah laughed as Oscar fed Mazie a piece of croissant.

"Nothing too interesting at the moment, just a few cheating spouses that I've got my eye on." Hannah winked at them. She loved the big cases, like solving murders. However, she was also grateful they didn't come up too often.

At that moment, the tinkle of the front door sounded and a man walked into the coffee shop. Hannah looked up to see a familiar face. Her eyes lifted in recognition, causing Oscar and Anita to turn and see who it was.

"Do you know him?" Anita asked.

"That's Frederick Hogan, Colin's accountant!" Hannah whispered. "I was just telling Colin how much I'd like to see him fall in love. He seems like such a sweet man."

Anita and Oscar exchanged a glance. "Do I sense that you may be launching a different kind of investigation on his behalf?" Anita joked.

"Frederick! Over here!" Hannah called.

The man's blue eyes lit up and he walked towards Hannah's table with a notable spring in his step. "Hi, Mazie," he said as he leaned down to say hello to the dog and scratch her belly. When he stretched back to standing the three others at the table were watching him. "Oh," he said, startled. "Yes, hello, Hannah." He looked around. "And..."

Hannah jumped in to introduce everyone. "These are my good friends, Oscar and Anita."

"Hello, there," he replied, his face slightly flushed.

"You seem in a very good mood today," Hannah said. "Anything special going on?"

Frederick's eyes flashed to her and he paused for a split second as if contemplating how to respond. Seeming to decide to go forward, the words came tumbling out of his mouth. "Oh, you noticed. Well," he scratched his neck, eyes darting to the table. "I've met someone." He looked for Hannah's reaction.

Hannah clapped her hands together. "Frederick, that is fantastic news! Who's the lucky woman?" she asked.

Frederick rushed ahead to tell her everything. "After I saw you and Colin, I left for a meeting with Lucas Blake. The meeting went well - and I mean very well." He paused to grin from ear to ear. "It yielded more than a new client. His granddaughter, Gloria, was also at the meeting." At the mention of Gloria's name, Hannah noticed his eyes dilate. "She was sitting at the table looking absolutely gorgeous. She was so stunning it was difficult to focus on the business with her grandfather, but somehow, I made it through. At the end of our time together, not only did Lucas offer me his account, but Gloria offered me her number!" Frederick took a step back as if to catch his breath. His face was flushed with excitement.

Hannah was watching him carefully and couldn't help but match his enthusiasm with her own. "Frederick! That is such fantastic news! I'm so, so thrilled for you! I can't think of a more deserving person to find love," she said.

Frederick brought a hand to his chest as if to still his beating heart. "Thank you, Hannah. That is a kind thing for you to say." He pushed his glasses up his nose. "We've spent almost every day together since we met, and I couldn't be happier. Things are going so well, I just didn't anticipate this romance, and can't believe how much we have in common," he said.

"I'm so happy for you," Hannah said.

Frederick's eyes seemed to light up. "In fact, Lucas is planning a party at his grand home. Why don't you come and bring Colin?" he asked.

"I love a party!" Hannah said. "I'll check with Colin, but I'm sure he'd be happy to join me. Just send me the details and we will be there!"

"It's all set then. I can't wait to introduce you both to Gloria," Frederick said. "Well, if you'll excuse me, I'm going to grab a strong cup of coffee so I can be sure to give Lucas's books the attention they deserve." He looked to Oscar and Anita. "It was lovely to have met you." Frederick smiled, his eyes twinkling as he turned to walk to the counter.

Hannah turned to her friends. "Well, that was much easier than I anticipated!"

Anita opened her mouth to respond when Oscar grabbed her arm and squeezed lightly, gesturing to Frederick. Anita nodded in return and waited until they were waving goodbye to him and he was safely outside the door.

"What was that all about?" Hannah asked them.

Anita lowered her voice. "Do you know anything about Gloria Blake?" she asked Hannah.

Hannah furrowed her brows slightly and shook her head. "Nothing more than Frederick just told us."

"I'll start by saying that Frederick was right in calling her gorgeous. She's tall, has long, butter-blonde hair, and her skin is like porcelain."

Hannah listened, wondering what the problem could be.

"She's glamorous, and when she is in the room, it's hard not to just stare at her." Anita looked at Hannah, waiting for a reaction.

Hannah looked to Oscar, hoping for some clarity.

Oscar coughed and jumped in. "Gloria is beautiful, there is no argument there," Oscar said. Then he lowered his voice and leaned closer to Hannah. "We've heard through the grapevine that she is a bit of a heartbreaker."

Hannah looked from Oscar to Anita. "Where have you heard this?"

"You'd be surprised at the information we get, just standing behind the counter. The folks who come in often forget we're there and talk to each other as if we can't hear what they are saying," Oscar said.

"More than one customer has come in talking about Gloria. And of course, she's come in herself. Which is how I know how stunning she is," Anita said.

"We are just wondering if Frederick knows who he's

dealing with," Oscar added. "Frederick seems lovely," Anita said. "But he's not exactly her usual type."

"Don't get me wrong, Frederick is not a bad-looking man!" Anita said. "However, Gloria goes through men pretty quickly, and we've never seen her in here with someone as..." she paused as if trying to find the right word to describe Frederick.

"Smart," Oscar said.

Anita nodded. "Yes, as smart as Frederick. It seems like there may be another motive for her pursuit of him."

Hannah finally understood what the pair had been trying to communicate with her. "You're saying that Gloria is a man-eater, and her type is usually a little taller, darker, and more handsome?"

"Classically handsome, immaculately dressed, with money to burn," Anita said. "Frederick is a very nice-looking man, it's just that Gloria usually has more of a wall street type on her arm... and less of an accountant type."

"I see," Hannah said. Her mind was churning, she could feel her investigative instincts kick into high gear. "Thank you so much for telling me, you two. I'm going to keep a sharp eye on them at Lucas Blake's party to determine if she has the right motivations with that sweet man."

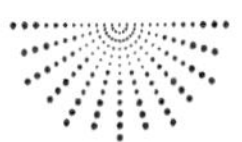

CHAPTER THREE

A few nights later, Hannah and Colin waited for the valet driver to take their keys as they sat in their car in front of the curved driveway of the grand Lucas Blake estate. "You look beautiful, as always, Hannah," Colin said, leaning over to kiss her cheek.

"Thank you, Colin. You clean up rather nicely yourself," she said, straightening the bow tie on his tuxedo. Her eyes traveled to his. "Remember, we need to watch Frederick and Gloria very closely."

Colin's eyes danced at her intensity. "Yes, we will watch them. Just remember that Frederick is a fully grown man, a successful one at that, and he can more than likely take care of himself," Colin replied.

"Yes, of course. Just keep an eye out to see if anything is off with them. You know? Like, watch to see how she looks at him, how much time they spend together, if they are touching each other equally."

Colin shook his head slightly. "Oh, to be in the mind of a woman!" he said. "I'll do my best, but I trust Frederick's judgment on this one."

Hannah seemed not to hear his last statement. "Thank you, honey. I'll be watching, too."

The valet came to take the keys to Colin's car, and the two of them approached the entrance, complete with a red carpet rolled out for guests leading to the front door. "Oh, this is fancy," Hannah said, squeezing herself closer to Colin.

They walked into Lucas Blake's luxurious home and took in the marble floors, the curved staircase, and the tall ceilings. The room was already filled with people in elegant evening wear, happily sipping on champagne and nibbling canapés. "This is so fun!" Hannah said.

Colin gave a slight nod across the room. "There they are."

Hannah followed his glance to see Frederick and Gloria standing close to one another beside the grand piano. Frederick was beaming, seeming to delight in being on Gloria's arm. Gloria, meanwhile, was as striking as Anita said she would be. She stood tall, slim, and poised; her figure tastefully highlighted under her custom gown in a deep burgundy. "Lucky Frederick," she whispered to Colin.

"Not as lucky as me," Colin whispered sending a shiver of delight down Hannah's spine.

The two of them made their way over to greet Frederick and Gloria. "Ah! You made it, so nice of you to come," Frederick said, greeting them. "This is my girlfriend, Gloria Blake." His smile overtook his face, he was filled with such joy.

"It's so nice to meet you, Gloria," Colin said, reaching to shake her hand.

"We have heard such nice things about you," Hannah said.

Gloria smiled at them both. "Same to you both. Frederick speaks highly of you, it's so nice to finally meet you," she said.

Hannah was impressed so far.

"Say, Frederick. I have a few questions for you about my accounts. I hate to mix business with pleasure, but would you mind if we spend a couple of minutes discussing it?" Colin asked. Hannah appreciated what he was doing, giving her time to talk to Gloria away from Frederick.

"Sure," Frederick replied good-naturedly. "Happy to."

Part of what made Hannah so successful at being an investigator was her willingness to ask tough and sometimes awkward questions. This was no exception. "So, Gloria. You and Frederick seem very happy."

Gloria smiled sweetly at Hannah. "We really are. I'm such a lucky lady."

Hannah matched her smile and continued. "As you can imagine I'm really protective of my friends, and I just want to be sure your intentions are pure."

Gloria's eyes flashed ever so slightly; you'd have missed it if you blinked. She gave no indication that this comment bothered her. "Of course," she said.

"I've heard that you have quite a history of dating and dumping men all down the East Coast. I'd like to be sure Frederick isn't going to be one left in your wake." Hannah held Gloria's gaze.

Gloria's chin tipped up ever so slightly. "I do indeed have a history, but it is just that: history. I have met a new man, Frederick. He's bringing out a new side of me, and I can assure you, you have nothing to worry about as it relates to me breaking his heart. If anything, I'm worried he's slightly out of my league!" Her eyes beamed, then she added, "Intellectually, of course."

"That is good to hear. Thank you for indulging my concerns," Hannah said.

"It is interesting that you're so overly concerned," Gloria said. "In fact, it makes me wonder if *you* have some interest in my boyfriend since you are so quick to lob such accusations in my direction."

Hannah felt herself jerk back. She had not been expecting this. "Of course, I don't have an interest in Frederick," she replied. "I'm happily dating Colin, whom you just met. I am more than content with my own romantic situation." Her hand was on her chest, affronted at the suggestion. Though shocked at the turn in the conversation, Hannah recognized it for what it was, a diversion. Gloria was trying to throw her off the scent of something, she just had to figure out what.

Before the air between them crackled with too much tension, they were joined by two others. One was a tall, blond man with the same blue eyes as Gloria, the other was a striking woman with raven-colored hair, mocha skin, and deep brown eyes. "Ah, Justin. Nice to see you, brother," Gloria greeted the man. "This is Hannah Barry."

Justin gave Hannah a curt nod.

"And this is my grandfather's former accountant, Pilar Morena," Gloria introduced the woman with less enthusiasm. With a dismissive gesture, she continued, "Emphasis on the word former. Right, Pilar? You've been informed that your services are no longer required. It's time for you to leave this party and this home... for good." Gloria stood with her arms crossed, daring Pilar to defy her.

"Gloria," Pilar said with an edge in her voice. "Don't do this. You can't do this!" Her volume increased, attracting the attention of those who stood around them.

Gloria gave a quick nod to two burly gentlemen standing close by with clear earpieces coiling down from their ears. They swiftly moved to take up positions on either side of Pilar, each gripping her upper arm, moving her toward the exit.

Pilar seemed confused by what was happening and began yelling. "I will not let Frederick get away with this! He will not get away with paving the way for his new girlfriend!" Her screeches echoed through the home as she was dragged out the side door.

Pilar's scene had the attention of the whole party. Everyone had stopped their conversations and turned to watch her wriggle under the secure grip of the security guards. Hannah watched as well, quickly searching for Frederick to see how he would react to such outlandish claims. She saw him move quickly across the room to stand by Gloria's side and comfort her. "Are you okay, darling?" he asked.

Gloria had been watching Pilar to ensure she was a safe distance away. When she saw her leave the house, she turned to Frederick. "I'm more than okay." She pulled Frederick in for a close embrace. Then she turned to the pianist whose fingers had frozen on the piano keys. "Let the dancing begin!" she called to him.

The pianist snapped out of his daze and his fingers danced over the keys, playing a rousing instrumental version of the latest hit pop songs. As the music floated through the air, Gloria wasted no time grabbing Frederick's hand and pulling him to the center of the room. She held both of his hands and encouraged him to move his body to the beat. Frederick, for all of his attempts, didn't seem to know how to feel the music. His body jerked wildly as he focused on Gloria. He seemed self-conscious about the crowd looking on and not at all comfortable being there.

Gloria took the lead, and they danced their way to the bar. Thrusting a shot of tequila in his hands she tipped it toward his mouth. "Drink up, it's a party!" she called. Frederick obeyed, and soon he was back on the dance floor, moving his body to the beat once again. He was no less awkward but seemed far less self-conscious by this point.

Hannah stayed in her same position where Justin

had also remained and the two of them watched the Gloria and Frederick show. Hannah seized the opportunity and turned to Justin. "Gosh, if I were Pilar, I might be upset too. What do you think, Justin? You two seemed pretty friendly when you came over here."

Justin sipped his champagne and replied while watching his sister dance in the middle of the room. "I honestly feel the same way that Pilar does. Since my sister's return, she's taken things over and has ruffled quite a few feathers around here."

"Interesting. Do you have any idea why Gloria is suddenly back in the picture? Why she seems intent on cozying up with your grandfather again?" Hannah asked.

Justin shook his head. "I've been wondering the same thing. It's been causing me concern." Then Justin spotted Lucas and walked over to speak with him. Hannah was sure to watch to see where they were heading so she could position herself to overhear their discussion.

Lucas and Justin went into Lucas's study and didn't close the door.

"What is it, Justin? There's a party for us to be enjoying out there," Lucas said.

"Grandfather, Pilar did not deserve to be fired, and I think you would have to agree with me on that," Justin said.

"Oh, I would, would I?" the older man replied.

"You used to trust my judgment implicitly until Gloria suddenly popped back into our lives," Justin said. "And it just so happens that she brought a new accountant with her? Don't you find that to be suspicious in any way?"

Hannah cringed at the whining tone that Justin took with his grandfather, wondering how the older gentleman would respond to it.

There was a moment before Lucas replied, then Hannah heard him cackle loudly and quite rudely. "Justin, my young grandson. Things always have a way of shifting. It would serve you well to remember that as you make the rest of your way through this life." Hannah heard footsteps approaching the door and she quickly busied herself with her phone, making it look like she'd stepped away from the party to make a phone call.

She watched as Lucas walked out of the study and back to the ballroom, never even noticing her.

Justin, meanwhile, was tossing papers and books around the study in defiance, obviously unhappy with the way things had just gone with his grandfather. Hannah chose that opportunity to return to Colin and report to him what she'd just heard.

Colin was casually leaning against the piano, enjoying watching the various people on the dance floor, when Hannah found him. "Colin!"

He turned to her and his eyes lit up. "Hannah, having fun?"

She moved closer to him. "I just overheard Justin and Lucas Blake talking in the study. I have a fear that something darker than I originally suspected might be at play." She looked up at him with concern in her chocolate brown eyes.

He leaned to kiss her forehead. "I have no doubt that you'll get to the bottom of it."

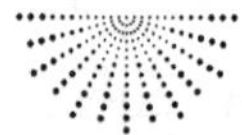

CHAPTER FOUR

Colin managed to convince Hannah to dance to a few songs with him, but her mind was still spinning with echoes of the conversation she'd eavesdropped on in the study. What could Lucas have meant when he said that things always have a way of shifting? Could it have been a simple warning to remain flexible? Why had Pilar been summarily dismissed? What brought Gloria back to town and why did her grandfather seem to favor her?

Colin did his best to help her take her mind off it, but she couldn't keep her eyes off of the dynamic between Gloria and Frederick. Every time the two of them danced past the bar, she'd offer him another drink, which Frederick quickly drank, and they'd carry on dancing. Sensing Hannah's fixation, he leaned to whisper in her ear. "Shall we call it a night?"

She looked up at him with gratitude pouring from her eyes. "Yes! I didn't know that's what I wanted until you just said it. I need a break from this night!" she said.

She and Colin retrieved his car from the valet and drove back to her place. "Why don't we take Mazie for a walk? That always seems to make you feel better," he said.

"That is a perfect idea," she said. "It makes both me and Mazie feel better."

They went into her house to find an excited Mazie, wagging her tail and waiting by the door. "Walk? Want to go for a walkie?" Hannah asked her dog, who replied by jumping around in a tight circle.

Hannah clipped the leash to Mazie's collar and the three of them were off to enjoy the fresh evening air. Hannah took a deep breath in and looked at the stars twinkling down at them from the clear blue sky. "I just wonder what Gloria is really up to," she said.

Colin laughed. "The walk isn't really working to take your mind off of it, is it?"

Her laugher joined his. "No, it's not. However, it's serving to provide some clarity for me…"

"Oh?" Colin asked.

"I'm wondering if Pilar's rage could explode into something even more dangerous. I feel like we haven't heard the last from her."

"She was pretty upset," Colin agreed.

The three of them walked around the streetlamp-lit town in happy silence, when Hannah felt a buzz in her pocket. "Hello?" she said into her phone's receiver.

Kate Carver's voice rang out on the speaker. Hannah looked to Colin with wide eyes when she recognized the chief of police's voice. "Hannah, I'm at the Blake home."

"Really? So sorry we missed you at the party, we just left!" she said.

"No, I'm here because we received a call about Lucas Blake. He has been found dead!"

"What?" Hannah replied. "Where did they find him?"

"Can you come over here? Right away? I'll fill you in on the details," Kate replied.

"I'm with Colin and Mazie, we'll be right there," Hannah said, hanging up the phone. Colin instinctively took Mazie's leash and started jogging, knowing Hannah would want to get to his car as quickly as possible. Mazie was thrilled at the increase in speed, her ears flopping naively behind her as she sped back in the direction they came.

When they arrived at Colin's car he asked, "Do you want to put Mazie back in?"

Hannah shook her head. "No time. Let's get to the Blake house!"

When they pulled the car around the curved driveway, this time there were no valet drivers to take their keys. They parked out of the way in case police cars and ambulances needed to get by and made their way into Lucas Blake's home for the second time that evening.

Kate was at the door to greet them. "Frederick is panicking, follow me."

Hannah hustled behind Kate, whose shorter legs did not stop her from moving them quickly. Kate led them to the same study Hannah had been eavesdropping in front of earlier that evening. Inside, what was presumably Lucas Blake's body was covered with a white sheet, and Frederick was pacing nervously back and forth behind the desk. He was biting his fingernails and his eyes were wildly scanning the room. His hair was disheveled, and his glasses were on Lucas's desk.

"Why is he fearful?" Hannah whispered to Kate.

"Frederick is the one who found Lucas's body," Kate replied. "I think it's safe to say he's still slightly intoxicated from the revelry of the evening. He says he cannot remember how he arrived in the study because he was so drunk. He also asked me to call you."

Mazie had been faithfully by Hannah's side up until now. She watched as her good friend, Frederick, seemed to be in emotional discomfort and broke away from Hannah's legs to rush over and comfort the man. She scampered behind the desk, reaching her front paws up on his legs.

The movement seemed to break Frederick from his confused trance, and he reached down to pat her head. "Oh, hi. It's you."

Gloria had been sitting quietly in a large, leather sitting chair watching her boyfriend pace the room. Hannah didn't notice her until she spoke. Her voice rose smooth and calm from the corner of the room. "Pilar must have sneaked back into the house and taken her revenge out on Lucas, who rightfully fired her," she said. "We all saw how enraged she was earlier this evening. Has anyone seen her?"

Hannah thought this was a good hypothesis.

Justin, who had left the study for a moment to get everyone some water came back in to hear Gloria's theory. He handed out the bottles, then looked to his sister. "That's a decent theory, sis, but I have a question for you. Where were you when Frederick discovered our grandfather? Isn't it a little bit convenient that your new boyfriend, whom you've been attached at the hip to all night, left your side for a split second, only to discover a dead body?" His eyes bored into his sister.

She stared back at him, unblinking.

"Seems to me that maybe you sent your accountant to deal with grandfather."

There was a moment's silence. "That makes no sense," Gloria finally responded. "I have no reason to send anyone to deal with Grandfather. We can all agree that he and I were on the same page about most things. Him dead is actually to my disadvantage."

Ralph Larson chose that moment to enter the study. His stocky frame filled the doorways. "Hey, boss, sorry it took me a while to get here, I was putting the baby to sleep," he said.

Kate looked relieved to have another person in uniform in the room. "No problem, Ralph. Would you do me a favor and search Mr. Blake's desk? It seems to me that might be the first place to look since this is the place he was killed."

A small, distressed moan escaped Gloria when she heard those words.

"Sure thing," Ralph said, moving to sift through the contents of Lucas's meticulously organized space. Everyone in the room watched as he took care to go through each piece of paper. It didn't take long before he drew in a sharp breath.

"What is it?" Kate asked.

He picked up the papers and walked them to the police chief.

She scanned them quickly, stopping to study the words carefully on the final page. She looked up at the eyes waiting for her announcement. "These papers say that in the event of Lucas Blake's murder the whole of his fortune is signed off to Frederick Hogan." He skipped through the pages. "They are signed by Frederick to say that he agrees." She looked at Frederick, still pacing behind the desk. At her announcement, he stopped cold. His face drained of all its color and he dropped his hands to his knees.

"That's impossible... I never saw or signed these," he managed to say through his dry mouth. "I'm in charge of his finances and I have never seen, nor heard of such a ludicrous contract. In fact, he and I have only just met! He would have been crazy to sign anything to me. My only role is to manage his money, not overtake it!" his tone raised in concern.

Ralph looked at Kate, who nodded in his direction. "Sorry, pal. We're going to have to take you in for questioning," Ralph said to Frederick.

Frederick looked to Gloria in desperation. She walked over to him and held his cheeks. "It's okay, Frederick. This will all be straightened out. Just answer their questions and everything will work itself out."

Frederick looked slightly mollified and let his shoulders drop in resignation. He seemed dazed, or maybe still drunk, but allowed Ralph to escort him to the police car. As he left, Mazie chased after him, whimpering.

Hannah called her dog back but couldn't help noticing that her puppy seemed more upset than Frederick's own girlfriend at the sight of him in handcuffs.

When Frederick was gone, Gloria turned to everyone in the room. "There is an explanation to all of this, we just need to find it."

"Where is this Pilar person everyone keeps mentioning?" Kate asked. "A few questions are floating around that it seems like only she can answer. Does anyone know where she went after she was escorted off the grounds this evening?"

Justin shook his head. "She was taken out so quickly I wasn't able to catch up with her. And she hasn't texted anything since she left."

"So, you have her number?" Kate asked.

"I do, here you go," Justin handed the police chief his phone.

As the discussion continued about Pilar, Hannah moved to look at the contents of Lucas's desk. She flipped through the contract he'd allegedly signed and had a thought. She waved the page with Frederick's signature in front of Mazie, who turned her nose up. *Strange,* Hannah thought. She thought Mazie would be much more interested, given how she all but ate Frederick's ink when they met at Troughton's Trough. She replaced the paper on the desk.

That settled it, Frederick was definitely being set up. Now, she needed to find out by whom.

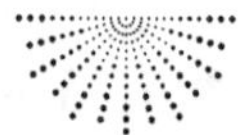

CHAPTER FIVE

The next day, Hannah's first stop was the police station. She convinced Kate to let her back to the cell where Frederick was being held so she could ask him a few questions. Given Hannah's history of helping Kate solve the local crimes, Kate knew it would be to her benefit.

Hannah approached the stark, grey cell to see Frederick languishing on his back, hand on his forehead as if to question how he got there in the first place.

"Hi, Frederick," she greeted the man.

Frederick jumped to sitting. "Hannah! Hello." His eyes fell to the floor, unable to meet hers.

"How are you feeling this morning?" she asked.

Frederick grimaced and rubbed his temples. "I can't believe I imbibed so heavily last night. That is totally unlike me. I don't think I've ever been that drunk before in my life."

"Hey, it happens to the best of us," Hannah replied. "I am guessing you were excited to be there with Gloria, maybe celebrating your new account, your new love? It could have happened to anyone."

Frederick's head lifted and his eyes softened. "I appreciate you saying that, Hannah. I can't tell you how embarrassed I am about my behavior."

Hannah noted that he seemed more concerned about his inappropriate behavior while inebriated than the threat of the murder charges hanging over him. "I wanted to ask you a few questions, Frederick."

"Ask me anything," he replied.

"What was the last thing you remember from last night?"

"I remember dancing with Gloria and taking drink after drink from the bar. I remember having a great time and thinking that it was very possible my life had been building up to that very moment," he said.

"So, no memory from the study?"

"None." He hung his head and frowned. "It would be fantastic if I had some recollection, for then I could come to my own defense in this terrible matter."

"About those papers?" Hannah asked.

"Those papers are falsified!" Frederick suddenly became very animated. "I had nothing to do with them. Mr. Blake and I never discussed anything even close to the idea that I may be the beneficiary of any of this wealth should he pass away. My business with him was purely professional." He looked to Hannah, his face practically begging her to believe him.

"When you sign documents do you always use your own pen, or would you use a pen offered to you?"

"Always my own. It's easier to get my signature uniform with the same pen and the same ink. I've been known to go back to the office if I ever forget it but now, I always have a pen on me." He patted his pocket as if looking for a pen. "Except for when I'm arrested for murder."

Although Hannah *did* believe him, she wanted to be crystal clear on the matter of his innocence. "To confirm, you swear that you never doctored any papers to make you the beneficiary of Lucas's financial holdings?"

"I swear it," he said solemnly. "I swear it on my life!"

Hannah nodded. "Okay, then. We are on the same page. Who do you think may have done it?"

Frederick straightened. "As you can imagine, I've been thinking a lot about this since I was locked in this cell. In fact, I've thought of nothing else. My suspicions lie with Pilar. I wonder if she was upset about being fired, with me in particular since I took her position. Perhaps she thought I had something to do with her being let go."

Hannah thought for a moment. "That theory makes a lot of sense to me, Frederick. It doesn't help that no one has been able to get a hold of her since she was escorted out of the party yesterday. She hasn't had a chance to provide an alibi."

"Maybe because she doesn't have one," Frederick said.

"Exactly."

"Hello, darling!" came a smooth voice from down the hallway.

Frederick brightened at the sound of his girlfriend's voice. "Gloria! You came to see me!" he called.

Hannah was disappointed to have been interrupted from their progress in brainstorming the killer. *He seems surprised to see her*, Hannah thought. *I would have thought he'd expect his girlfriend to visit him in jail after being wrongly accused of killing her own grandfather.* Nevertheless, she stepped back to allow them to visit.

"Thanks for the chat, Frederick. I'll be in touch," she said.

Gloria briefly looked at Hannah and gave her a dismissive smile before speaking to her boyfriend.

Outside the police station, Colin and Mazie were waiting for Hannah to finish talking with Frederick. Colin decided to stay outside and enjoy the sunshine while she spoke with the temporary prisoner. Hannah also didn't want Mazie to get too upset seeing Frederick behind bars. "We need to find Pilar," she said to Colin.

"Okay, then! How do you propose we do that?" he asked. "Hasn't Kate been looking for her?"

"No one has heard from her, but we need to change that. I'm not convinced she was the killer, but I do think she knows more than she's said so far. It felt as if her outburst at the party was stemming from something deeper than having been fired," Hannah said.

"Where should we look first?" Colin asked.

"She's not at home, and she doesn't have a job right now, so presumably she's low on cash," Hannah thought aloud.

Colin nodded along.

"Which means that she's either at a friend's place or the cheapest motel in the area."

"We know that Kate has called all her family and friends so far, to no avail," Colin said.

"Which leaves the motel down the road," Hannah said in triumph.

Colin grinned. "Hop in the car, let's pay this Pilar a visit," he said.

Mazie wagged her tail in agreement, hopping up onto Hannah's lap in the passenger seat.

Hannah, Colin, and Mazie stood outside the paper-thin door of room 111 at a shabby hotel just outside of town. The chipping maroon paint shook as they knocked on the door. The man at the front desk confirmed that a woman with raven hair had checked in last night, and told them which room she was in without even asking for a reason. Maybe, it was the $100 bill that Colin had produced!

They waited a moment for an answer, then tried again. Hannah leaned her ear against the door, trying to determine if she could hear anything on the other side. Then Mazie jumped up on her hind legs, yapping loudly.

Hannah put a finger in her ear. "If she won't open the door to get Mazie to stop, she might really not be here," she said. Not long after Mazie began barking, someone unseen turned the knob. Pilar peeked one of her deep brown eyes out the small crack she'd opened. "What do you want?" she asked in a husky voice that sounded as if she'd been crying.

"Thank you for answering the door, Pilar," Hannah said. "We only want to ask you a few questions." Hannah had her hands up in surrender, trying to convince the woman they meant no harm.

Pilar seemed convinced and opened the door fully. "Come in," she said.

Hannah, Colin, and Mazie filed into the room. The two humans stood respectfully near the door, hoping to help put Pilar at ease, while Mazie ran to sniff Pilar's legs. The nervous woman watched with wide eyes until Mazie evidently had enough and settled into a sleeping ball in the nearest corner.

The unexpected ceremony caused Hannah to glance quickly at Colin, who gave a subtle wink in return.

"I'll get right to the point," Hannah said. "How did it come that you were fired from your job working for Lucas Blake?"

Pilar's face paled as she reached to open the drawer of the bedside table. She pulled out a letter. "This is a document detailing supposed inaccuracies in the books I'd been keeping for Lucas," she said, handing them to Hannah. "As you can see, the report was signed by Frederick Hogan. He wrote a whole letter about my ineptitude as an accountant." Pilar's eyes clouded in anger.

"So, you were fired because Frederick exposed issues with your accounting?" Hannah asked.

"That's correct."

"Did this letter anger you?" Hannah asked, surprised at the turn of events.

Pilar narrowed her gaze at Hannah. "I know what you're getting at. Of course, this letter fueled my rage at Frederick."

Colin couldn't help but jump in. "Is that why you killed Lucas and set Frederick up for the fall?" he asked, his face flushed with excitement.

Pilar's mouth dropped. "What? Of course not! I said I was upset by it. As anyone would be. Being angry doesn't mean I would kill someone!" she exclaimed.

Hannah watched the exchange, unsure of what to think. Then she took the letter with Frederick's signature on it and waved it in Mazie's direction. Mazie roused slightly to see what the commotion was, took a small sniff of the air, and went right back to her nap.

"I believe you, Pilar," Hannah said.

Pilar stopped waving her hands in mid-air. "Wait, you do?"

Hannah nodded, "I do. I know this is scary for you, but please trust me on this. I need you to sit tight and wait for me to put the missing pieces together. I'll be in touch," she said, rubbing Pilar's arm in comfort.

Colin's mouth hung open slightly. He'd never seen Hannah make a statement like that without having peppered the suspect first with dozens of questions.

They said their goodbyes and got back into his car. Colin looked over at his girlfriend to ask, "What made you suddenly land on Pilar's side?"

Hannah rubbed Mazie's soft head just behind her ears in appreciation before she responded. "Mazie was uninterested in the smell of the paper. Remember at your restaurant that day she met Frederick? We were worried she would get ink poisoning; she was so intrigued by the smell of his pen that she wouldn't stop licking the paper?" she asked.

Colin nodded. "I remember."

"Frederick only uses that pen to sign his important documents. That letter would certainly be classified as one. The same goes for the papers found in Lucas's study, indicating that Frederick would be the beneficiary in the event of his death. Frederick didn't sign either one of those documents, they are an obvious forgery," Hannah said. She could feel her heart race as she reported this to Colin.

He whistled in appreciation. "Wow, Hannah. Nice detective work! So, who's this forger?" he asked.

She reached up to give him a quick kiss on the cheek. "We are one step closer to finding out."

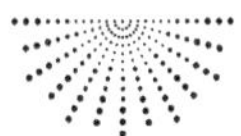

CHAPTER SIX

Hannah and Colin made their way back from the motel to the Blake estate. When they arrived, they saw Gloria's car. They approached the grand entrance and knocked on the door. Sure enough, the tall, blonde woman was there to greet them.

Gloria gave Hannah a once-over. "Twice in one day, how lovely," she scoffed. "How may I help you?"

Hannah squared her shoulders and looked Gloria in her eyes. "We came to ask you a few questions," she said.

"Fine, ask away." Gloria crossed her arms over her chest and raised her chin.

Hannah wasted no time jumping into the tough questions. "What brought you back to town after so long?" she asked.

Gloria's gaze remained hard.

"Why did you suddenly reappear in Lucas's life?" Hannah continued asking another pointed question that caused Gloria to flutter her lashes. Hannah noted the slight tell.

"Why, he's my grandfather, of course. I love him dearly. It's only natural to return to one's home. He was obviously getting older and I wanted to establish a meaningful bond with the man... before it was too late," she said and sniffed as if biting back tears.

"Hmm," Hannah replied.

If Gloria felt intimidated, she did not show it.

"My understanding is that you returned a few times to 'establish a bond', as you say. Why did you keep leaving if you were so intent on getting to know your grandfather?"

Gloria's arms gripped tighter around her chest, but her face gave nothing away. "If you are questioning why a granddaughter would want to get to know her grandfather, then I'm afraid you may need to change careers. This line of questioning will not get you to the bottom of any murder."

Hannah knew what Gloria was trying to do and did not let her attempt to undermine her skills bother her so she pressed on. "What about Frederick?" Mazie barked excitedly at the mention of his name, Hannah bit back a smile and continued. "He's not the type of man you usually go for, is he?" Hannah watched for any more reaction from Gloria. She saw nothing but a stone-cold face. "What exactly attracted you to him?" Hannah asked.

Gloria smiled. "Frederick? Why he's an absolute gem of a man. What's not to love about him? Even you, as I've mentioned before, seem to find him endearing." Gloria cast a suggestive glance in Colin's direction, no doubt hoping to cast doubt in his mind about Hannah's loyalties.

Hannah smiled, ignoring her attempt at a diversion. "That's not exactly an answer, though, is it?"

Gloria placed all her weight on one hip. "Your line of questioning seems vague at best. You seem to be pulling at arbitrary straws and you are now officially wasting my time. Are we done here?" she asked.

"Not quite," Hannah replied. She reached into her purse and pulled out the letter Pilar had given her at the motel. "Have you seen this document before?"

Gloria narrowed her eyes at the letter, then held her hand out. Hannah gave it to her and watched as she read it over. "I've never laid a single eye on these pages in my life," she said finally.

Hannah scrutinized the woman, looking for some sort of telltale sign to determine if she was speaking the truth or telling lies. There was nothing.

Gloria slowly lifted her gaze to meet Hannah's, a spark forming in her eyes. "This does suggest something rather sinister, however," she said.

"Oh? What's that?" Hannah asked.

"It suggests that Pilar is, in fact, guilty of murdering my grandfather," she said. Gloria seemed very satisfied with this statement.

Hannah put her hand out to indicate that Gloria needed to slow down with the accusation. "Not so fast. We have a few more leads to track down before we can make a definite statement like that."

Gloria clutched her chest. "That's what you may think, but I, for one, am fearful that the woman is unhinged. What happens if she isn't satisfied with the death of just my grandfather and wants to go after his next heir? Why, she'll no doubt target me, or my brother next!" Her voice lifted in concern, then she began weeping, right there.

Colin nudged Hannah's arm, and Hannah looked up to exchange a glance. Gloria transitioned to crying without any notice at all.

Through Gloria's tears, she managed to add, "I can't stand to think that Frederick is suffering on account of his love for me!" she said. "That poor, sweet man."

Hannah surpassed an eye-roll before comforting the woman. "Gloria, keep the faith." Hannah patted Gloria's back. "I have reason to believe that Frederick is not the person who signed the letter."

Gloria's sobs stopped abruptly. She peeked at Hannah through her fingers.

"I also believe the letter is a forgery," Hannah continued.

Gloria's hands dropped. "What makes you think that?" she asked, the look of surprise was easy to discern.

"Only the true culprit knows the full truth, but don't worry, I intend to discover who that might be," Hannah said. "We'll leave you to it, then. Colin and I are going to continue the investigation." Hannah waved at the woman and turned to walk back toward her car.

Gloria seemed startled at their abrupt departure but covered it up by calling after them. "Goodbye, then. Thank you for dropping by. And do keep me informed of your discoveries!"

Mazie turned to growl at the woman in the form of goodbye. "Good doggy," Hannah said, patting Mazie's bottom in an attempt to hurry her along to the car.

After the three of them were back and settled in Colin's vehicle and they'd made sure the windows were rolled up tightly and the doors secured, Colin spoke. "Do you think Gloria may have forged the letter in Lucas's study?"

Hannah shrugged. "It's a definite possibility, but it's too soon to say."

"It seems likely that she may have tried to do so, in order to get her hands-on her grandfather's fortune," he said.

"If so, she used the wrong ink and that was ultimately her downfall," Hannah replied. "However, it certainly would explain her sudden return to Blairstown and the reignited interest in her grandfather."

"The timing is also suspicious," Colin added. "She came back to town and suddenly not only did Pilar get fired, but her grandfather was killed. If it's a coincidence, which it doesn't seem to be, it's an awful unfortunate one."

Hannah agreed. "Even Mazie doesn't have a good feeling about Gloria," she said.

Mazie growled at the mention of Gloria's name in the same sentences as her own, causing Hannah and Colin to share a laugh.

"What do you say we grab a bite to eat?" Colin suggested. "The restaurant is serving my favorite linguini this evening. We can get you some brain food, so you are more than ready to crack this case tomorrow." They looked out the window to see the setting sun casting a burnt orange across the sky.

Hannah placed a hand on her stomach. "I'd love that," she replied. "I'm not sure there is much more for us to do at this hour anyway, but with a good meal and a full night's sleep, we can be up bright and early tomorrow," she said.

"To Troughton's Trough, then?" Colin confirmed.

Mazie heard the name of her favorite restaurant and let out a yelp, followed by her tail wagging furiously.

Hannah chuckled. "Looks as though we are all in agreement."

Hannah, Colin, and Mazie enjoyed a delicious meal at Troughton's Trough, each returning home to have a sound sleep before another day of discovery began.

CHAPTER SEVEN

Hannah woke with the birds the next morning and was enjoying a steaming cup of coffee on her front porch when a call came in from Kate Carver.

"Hello?" Hannah answered.

"Morning, Hannah," Kate said. "Justin has come to the police station. I think you should come down here to see what he has to say."

"Thanks for the call," Hannah replied. "I'll take Mazie for a walk and we'll end at the station. I'd like to get a lay of the land."

"Great, see you soon," Kate said.

Hannah and Mazie took the direct path to the station, rather than meandering around their usual walk. Mazie seemed to sense the urgency and didn't insist on stopping to smell each and every bush like she usually did. The two of them arrived in record time. Hannah approached the front desk just as the police chief was coming down the corridor.

"Hannah! Come on back here. Please join me in my office, if you don't mind."

Hannah and Mazie followed behind as Kate's short legs walked swiftly through the halls. When they arrived at her office, sitting and waiting in the chairs across from Kate's desk was Gloria's brother, Justin. Ralph was standing guard, watching Justin carefully with his arms in front of him.

Kate moved behind the desk and motioned for Hannah to sit in the open seat.

Justin sighed impatiently. "As I was saying, I'm going to hire a proper lawyer for Frederick. He deserves a fair defense, and from what I can see, my sister is setting the poor fellow up for forgery and the murder." He shook his head in disgust.

"Shall we bring Frederick into the room?" Kate asked him.

"A fantastic idea," Justin replied.

Kate nodded for Ralph to go retrieve the prisoner. Frederick appeared in the doorway not very long after they heard his footsteps shuffle down the hallway. Ralph held his handcuffed wrists as he escorted him to a seat.

Hannah glanced at his orange jumpsuit in sympathy. This was not a man who deserved to be locked up, in her opinion.

Justin turned to Frederick. "I'm going to get you a real lawyer and get you out of here," he repeated.

Frederick's eyes lit up. "You are? Oh, thank you, Justin. I can't say how much that means to me."

"Listen to me, pal," Justin said to Frederick. He leaned closer to the man, while Frederick's eyes flashed with worry and he leaned away from Justin. "The timing of my grandfather hiring you is suspicious. The fact that you were hired and then suddenly started dating Gloria, right before he died, leaving his estate to you?" Justin paused and blew a big breath out. "You'd have to be an idiot not to suspect the woman." His eyes lingered on Frederick as if to challenge him to argue.

Frederick leaned forward and opened his mouth to speak, but Justin continued without allowing him to start. "It was all engineered so that Gloria could kill Lucas, and *not* seem like the prime suspect."

Frederick stared back at the man, shifting in his seat uncomfortably. He began to speak again, his trembling voice betraying his nerves. "Gloria would never do such a thing," he said.

Justin sighed and hung his head.

Frederick seemed to gain some confidence and raise his voice slightly, saying the words once more. "Gloria - your sister - would never do such a thing!" he said.

Justin stood up from his seat. "You poor fool," he said as he left the room without even looking back.

Hannah cast a glance at Kate. "I'm going to follow him. I want to ask him a few more questions," she said. His exit was so swift, she realized she hadn't had a chance to ask him anything yet.

Kate nodded. "Sure thing, just call me after."

Hannah wrapped Mazie's leash around her hand and patted Fredrick on the shoulder before moving swiftly out the door, hoping she hadn't lost her chance to find Justin. She saw him headed for this truck in the parking lot. "Justin!" she called after him.

The blond man turned, his ice-blue eyes finding her. Hannah was struck with his resemblance to his sister. "I have a few more questions for you... if you don't mind," she said.

He stopped and waited. "What's up?"

She and Mazie caught up and Hannah continued carefully. "I know you think your sister is guilty of setting Frederick up for the crimes she committed," she began.

Justin nodded enthusiastically; seemingly happy someone was on his side.

"These cases often come down to proof. Even if you are correct, it would be hard to convict her without evidence. Besides her sordid reputation, do you have anything that would definitively prove Gloria's guilt?" Hannah asked him.

Justin shook his head. "I'm afraid I don't. But given her history, I'm surprised that's not enough. She is always doing this. She leaves town, forgets about her family, no one hears from her for months or even years, and then she reappears with no warning. Each time, she manages to weasel her way back into our grandfather's life. Each time he thinks she has changed and begins to trust her, and she repeatedly loses his trust." Justin looked pained. "Only this time, she did more than lose his trust. She lost his life."

Hannah studied him carefully. "Sounds like a complicated family dynamic," she said.

Justin had been looking at the ground, then his eyes flashed to hers. "I'm tired of the whole rotten thing, to be honest."

"I can imagine," Hannah replied.

"I'm going to head out on my uncle's boat this afternoon. I need to clear my head, think about things, and try to calm down," Justin said, reaching a hand to open his truck door.

"That sounds nice," Hannah replied. "Good luck with that."

Justin silently climbed into the cab of his truck and drove off.

Hannah, meanwhile, wanted to go back to visit with Pilar. She used the walk back to her place as an opportunity to clear her own head. When she arrived, she thought she had a plan. She and Mazie hopped into her car and headed to the motel just out of town.

She knocked on room 111 and waited. This time Pilar came much more quickly. "Who is it?" she called from behind the door.

"It's Hannah and Mazie!"

Pilar opened the door right away. "Come in. Tell me what's new," she said.

Hannah settled herself on the end of Pilar's crisply made bed. "I was just able to speak with Justin. He told me that he is going to hire Frederick a good lawyer to help get him off. He is insistent that it was Gloria who forged the documents, and killed their grandfather," Hannah reported. "He also mentioned that Gloria caused some difficult family dynamics with her constant departures and returns, confusing Lucas Blake and making waves for everyone else. Especially Justin."

Pilar agreed. "There is some truth to his story. Lucas was not an easy man to work for. Don't get me wrong, it's an absolute tragedy that he was murdered, but he didn't necessarily leave a host of friends in his wake," she said.

"What about Gloria, did you know her very well?" Hannah asked.

"Not well, no. As Justin mentioned, she came and went pretty frequently. I think he was likely correct in assuming she would come back to try and get in Lucas's good graces. I'm also guessing that she'd leave so soon afterward because Lucas was such a difficult man to be around," she hypothesized.

"What about Justin?" Hannah asked. "He stuck around the whole time."

"He did. I don't want to put words into his mouth or anything, but I'd assume that was his way of attempting to stay in Lucas's good graces," Pilar said.

"Did it seem that Lucas had a favorite?" Hannah asked.

"Well, that was part of his charm," Pilar said. "Lucas refused to name an official heir to his fortune. And he did it just to keep Gloria and Justin on their toes. I can understand wanting to keep them working hard but it did more than that - it caused a lot of drama and uneasy feelings between them."

Hannah hung onto every word Pilar was saying. "Pilar, this is such helpful information, thank you for telling it to me."

"It's the least I can do," she replied. "Especially if I want to prove my innocence."

Hannah folded her hands together in front of her. "Pilar, I have an idea."

"I love ideas," Pilar replied.

"It's going to require you to go out on a long limb and put your trust in me, however," Hannah said, a warning look in her eye.

Pilar stared at Hannah, waiting for the bomb to drop.

"Would you trust me enough to go to the police station?" Hannah asked tentatively.

Pilar openly balked. "The police station?"

Hannah nodded.

"What, to turn myself in?" she asked.

"No, not to turn yourself in for arrest," Hannah said. "Just to go in and be willing to submit to questioning. I really think that if Kate heard your side of things, it would help clear your name." Hannah thought she saw Pilar soften to the idea and went in for the kill. "Right now, your silence is speaking volumes, but it's saying all the wrong things."

Pilar tilted her head to the side as if to ponder the suggestion.

"Trust me. I'm on your side in this."

"Well, I guess I don't really have another option at the moment," Pilar replied. "This might come back to bite me, but I feel like I can really trust you."

Hannah grabbed Pilar's hand to squeeze it. "You really can."

Mazie, who had been sitting quietly at the foot of the

bed yapped in agreement. Pilar jumped in surprise and looked at the dog, while Hannah laughed. "Sounds like Mazie thinks it's a good idea," she said.

"Okay, then." Pilar threw her shoulders back and lifted her chin. "It is decided. I'll go to the police station."

"You won't regret this," Hannah said.

Pilar whispered. "I just hope you know what you are doing."

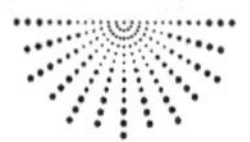

Pilar and Hannah drove to the police station in companionable silence. Pilar was playing with her raven hair, pulling it up to a ponytail and taking it down again. She repeated this over and over. Hannah chalked it up to nerves and recommitted to herself that she would not let the woman down.

When they walked into the station, Kate was shocked. "Is this the one and only Pilar Moreno?" she asked. "Wherever did you find her?"

Hannah could sense Pilar go rigid beside her and didn't want to embarrass her, so she decided to gloss over the old motel part of the story. "Pilar came of her own accord and is willing to answer any of your questions about both Lucas Blake and the night he was murdered."

Kate looked impressed. "Well, thank you for coming in today, Pilar. Please, come this way so we can ask you about the night in question." She thanked Hannah for her help and led Pilar down the hallway. Hannah chose to wait at the station to hear what Kate thought about her conversation with Pilar. She waited outside with Mazie, enjoying the fresh air when - to her surprise - Frederick walked out of the station doors.

"Frederick!" she greeted him. "They released you?"

Mazie turned to see who Hannah was speaking to and when she recognized Frederick, she all but jumped into his arms.

Frederick looked wild-eyed and squinted at the bright sun. When he recognized Mazie, he relaxed, kneeling down to pet her head. "They did," he said, looking up to Hannah. "They came into my cell and told me I was off the hook."

"Did they say why?" Hannah asked him.

"They didn't. To be honest, I was so relieved to be

free that I didn't want to ask too many questions in case they changed their mind. They were very clear that they didn't want me to leave town, so I'll be in the area," he said. Frederick shifted from left to right, his eyes darting around the parking lot. "I do feel bad that it seems Pilar has taken my place in there. I'm not sure she deserves to be in the hot seat, but I do need to get back to Gloria." A yellow taxi pulled up in front of the curb.

Hannah could sense that he was anxious to leave, so she wrapped up the conversation. "Well, I'm glad you're no longer falsely behind bars. Please watch who you talk to and I'll see you around."

"Bye, Hannah," Frederick said. "Thanks for finding Pilar." He gave Mazie one last scratch behind her ears and got in the back of his waiting taxi.

Hannah watched as Frederick's taxi made its way to see Gloria and placed a quick call to Colin. She was ready to execute the next part of her plan.

Then she led Mazie on a walk in the direction of the dock where she was hoping to find Justin. She spotted him on a beautiful, expensive ski boat and walked to the end of the quay to flag him down.

When she waved both hands in the air, Mazie began barking as well, causing him to look and see what the commotion was.

She watched as Justin squinted his eyes and pointed to himself. "Me?" she heard him call out.

"Yes! Justin!" Hannah replied. "Would you come to the dock? I have found Pilar!" she yelled back.

Justin seemed to register what she said and redirected the boat back to shore. He pulled the boat up and tied it quickly. "Hey, Hannah." He hopped off and stood in front of her, his eyes lit with anticipation. "What's this about finding Pilar?" he asked.

"Pilar went in for questioning at the station, and she's now in custody," Hannah replied. "As a result, Frederick was released and is now on his way to meet Gloria."

Justin's eyebrows lifted. "Oh?"

Hannah continued to share the story about the faulty ink. "We now know that Frederick's pen uses a very distinctive ink, so we know that the documents found on Lucas's desk were definitely falsified."

Justin listened carefully.

"It made me wonder if Gloria will be quick to forge other documents in a bid to secure Lucas's fortune, especially now that Frederick is out of jail," Hannah finished.

Justin reached his hand out to shake Hannah's. "I am so appreciative that you have kept me in the loop, Hannah. Thank you for this update. After what I've heard, I need to go call my grandfather's lawyer again to see what my next step should be," he said. He pumped Hannah's hand twice, confidently and with a firm grip, then left to get in his truck.

Hannah and Mazie watched as he hurried away from the dock. Hannah stooped to scratch Mazie's ears, then whispered to her. "Have your nose at the ready, Mazie. We're going to need it soon." She slipped a treat out of her pocket and fed it to her dog. Then she placed a call to Kate.

Hannah and Mazie took another leisurely walk back to her place; Mazie was thoroughly happy with the exercise she'd received already that day. An hour later, the two of them hopped in the car to the Blake estate. They stayed parked out front until they saw

Justin rushing by them, run to the front of the house, and disappear behind the large, imposing door.

Mazie pawed at the window and Hannah patted her head. "Not quite yet, Mazie," Hannah said, waiting a minute before they got out of the car.

Once they did make their way to the entrance, the door was left ajar, so Hannah let herself in. She saw Gloria and Frederick sitting next to one another in the sitting room. Mazie recognized her good friend immediately and scampered over, jumping up to sit on Frederick's lap.

"Hey, Mazie!" he called, nuzzling her face with his.

Gloria gave the two of them the side-eye and scooted away slightly.

Something caught the corner of Hannah's eye, and she looked to see that it was Justin waving another letter in his hands. He was coming down the hall from the direction of Lucas's office. "This is proof!" he called.

Frederick and Gloria looked up to see why Justin was yelling. "This is the proof that I am the heir apparent! I finally found it," he said.

Gloria and Frederick looked alarmed. "What are you talking about?" Gloria asked. She stood up from the couch to approach Justin.

He showed her the signed documentation. "This is a letter signed by grandfather, indicating that he left the family fortune to me. *Not* you." He sneered at her. "So much for you waltzing back into town, trying to get him in your good graces. And so much for your failed attempts at forging the first letter."

Gloria's faced reddened in anger. "How dare you accuse me of such a thing," she hissed. "I did nothing of the sort."

"Yeah, right. I know the truth. I've solved this whole mess. You, dear sister, seduced Frederick here, you were probably going to go as far as to marry him, even. All so that you could forge documents and convince not only yourself but everyone else that he loved you best," Justin said.

Frederick gently moved Mazie to the side and stood up to take his place beside Gloria. "I resent such an accusation, on behalf of our love for one another," he said. "Gloria and I are madly in love. Any union between the two of us will come as a result of romance, not finance." He looked pleased with his show of chivalry.

"Ha! Nice try. No one is buying your act, you two," Justin said. "The entire scheme is futile!" he said, still waving the papers around wildly.

Mazie was watching the exchange from the couch, sniffing the air. Finally, she hopped off the couch and ran toward Justin, sniffing the air as she went. When he didn't pay her any attention, Mazie lifted her front paws and hopped on her hind legs. She was sniffing and jumping, trying to reach the pages.

Hannah noticed what was happening. The papers were signed with Frederick's special ink!

Frederick recalled Mazie's excitement for his ink at Troughton's Trough and seemed to also piece together what was going on. He met Hannah's eyes and lifted his eyebrow as if to ask her a silent question. *How could his ink have been used on the pages, when he had been in police custody for the better part of the day?*

Hannah nodded at Frederick and marched over to Justin. "What a relief that you've gotten to the bottom of this mystery!" Hannah said. "I'd like to take a look at those papers," she said, reaching for the documents Justin had been waving around.

Justin handed them to her, willingly.

Hannah examined the papers closely, flipping from one to the next. When she arrived at the signature at the back, she sniffed the ink herself. Mazie was jumping at her legs, hoping for a sniff herself.

"This looks authentic, Justin," Hannah said.

Justin looked very satisfied at her response. Until she continued.

"There is just one small issue. There is no way Frederick could have affixed his signature to this piece of paper." She watched Justin for his reaction.

Justin scoffed. "Oh, really? What makes you say that?" he asked.

"To begin with, I have it on good authority that Lucas Blake was not in the habit of willing his money to either one of you. He famously refused to put either one of you in the will in order to keep you on your toes," she said.

"Nonsense," Justin said. "I don't know who you heard that from, but it's a complete lie. I spent every single day with Lucas, and he and I had many conversations about who his money would be willed to." Justin looked at her in defiance.

"That is interesting to hear," Hannah said. "Especially because Pilar let me know that he had spoken with her at length indicating quite the contrary."

Justin's fists clenched. "And that is exactly the reason

why she was fired!" he yelled, taking an intimidating step closer to Hannah.

"Is that right?" came a voice from the doorway. Everyone turned to see to whom it belonged. There, standing beside Ralph, who was holding her arm, was Pilar Moreno.

"Lucas Blake did not have a will. He and I discussed this many times," she announced.

Hannah briefly closed her eyes, relieved that her plan had worked.

Frederick stood looking confused, glancing between Pilar, Justin, and Gloria, obviously hoping for some kind of clarity.

Hannah stepped forward. "Allow me to provide some clarity, Frederick."

He turned to hear what she had to say.

"I think Gloria here did, in fact, forge the first letter found on Lucas's desk," Hannah said.

Gloria's hand moved to the side of her cheek, her jaw dropping. "How dare you!" she said

Hannah continued. "I also think she planned to

marry Frederick," Gloria's face turned up in a satisfied smile at this, "...in order to secure her piece of the pie," Hannah finished.

"Who exactly do you think you are? Coming here into my grandfather's home, spreading your lies, absolutely uninvited?" Gloria said, grabbing Frederick's arm and moving closer to him.

"I'm not quite finished," Hannah continued, undeterred by the woman's objections. "It's my opinion that you would not have killed Lucas."

Gloria's face morphed from being horrified to looking rather smug. "Exactly," she said.

"I do think you were the one who orchestrated it so that Pilar was pushed out, and Frederick was moved in," Hannah narrowed her eyes at Gloria, who simply shrugged in response. "However, there's no way you would have killed Lucas without a ring on your finger."

Gloria didn't know what to say to this, while Frederick pushed his glasses up, looking both offended and as though he was still trying to catch up and figure everything out.

All eyes were still on Hannah, so she continued her theory. "Going back to the night of the party. It's my opinion that *Justin* is the one who snapped in the wake of Lucas's dismissive words. Causing him to react by murdering his own grandfather." Hannah let out a breath after dropping that bomb on the room and surveyed the faces looking at her for their reactions.

Justin, who had been looking rather sure of himself up until this point turned stone cold. "Frederick was with me! He's my alibi, I did no such thing!" he argued.

Hannah grimaced. "That may be true, but the fact that Frederick was too drunk to recall how he made his way into the study is simply a bonus. Frederick isn't able to reliably tell anyone where he was or what he was doing that night. Unless there are other eye-witnesses."

"His irresponsible drinking is not my issue," Justin said.

"On that, I'd disagree," Hannah said. "Your little plan might have worked if Gloria had used

Frederick's preferred brand of ink. Unfortunately, she led you astray on that."

It was Gloria's turn to object to this comment and began sighing and rolling her eyes.

"I don't know what makes you say that because it's obvious that Frederick's ink was used on those pages," Justin pointed to the papers Hannah was holding.

Hannah nodded. "You have a point there. These documents are, in fact, signed using Frederick's ink. There's only one problem. One moment please," Hannah pulled out her phone and dialed Colin's number, putting him on speakerphone for all to hear his voice.

"Colin? Hello. Can you tell me and everyone listening where you were this afternoon?" Hannah asked.

"Hi, Hannah. You called me after you saw Justin at the dock. He said he was going to pay his lawyer a visit. Well, I followed him, per your instructions, and Justin did not, in fact, seek out his lawyer," Colin's voice said.

Hannah cast a glance around the room. "Did you follow him to his actual destination?" Hannah asked.

"I did. Justin actually went to Frederick's office. Once there, he jimmied the lock to his office to get his hands-on Frederick's special ink," Colin said.

Justin's ice blue eyes suddenly went wild. He scanned the room, his eyes settling on the nearest exit. "He can't prove that I stole a pen!" Colin tried in desperation to change the narrative. "I had to get into Frederick's office because I forgot something!" he yelled.

Ralph released Pilar's arm and slowly walked toward Justin.

Justin saw him coming and took a step back. "Hannah, you are a meddling, no-good, wanna-be P.I.! You don't know what you are doing, this is a hatchet job!" he screamed. Then he looked to his sister. "Gloria, you are a gold-digging, manipulative granddaughter, and Lucas never really loved you!" he yelled.

At this, Ralph grabbed his arm and clipped his wrists behind him in handcuffs. "Let's go down to the station," he said to Justin.

Once Justin had left the room, Frederick's energy seemed to leave him all at once and he collapsed back into the couch behind him. Gloria looked around the room, trying to get a gauge of the mood. Then she turned to her boyfriend and sat next to him on the couch, cozying her body close to his. She began stroking her hand along his back. Hannah thought it looked like she was trying to take his mind off the fact that she had just forged his name on some documents.

Frederick pushed his glasses up his nose and took a deep breath. "So, what's going to happen to Lucas's fortune? Are there any legitimate papers indicating who is the ultimate heir?"

Everyone looked to Pilar to answer this, as she had been in charge of the finances before all of the forgeries began appearing.

"There is no real will," Pilar answered. "Lucas didn't leave his money to anyone. His fortune does not have a home." She looked at Frederick. "Unless, of course, you did sign anything legitimately before he passed away?"

Frederick shook his head. "No, I did not. We never

discussed that part of his finances. We focused only on the business end," he replied.

Gloria looked dismayed. Her mouth hung open slightly as she listened to the accountants talk. "So, what will happen to his fortune then?" she asked.

Pilar answered, "It will likely go into probate first, then be dispersed among his favorite charities."

Gloria let out a disgusted tsk. "Unbelievable," she muttered.

Frederick turned to his girlfriend. "Darling, I'm still happy to have you. The money never mattered to me. Plus, you don't have to worry about money. I'll share all that I have," he looked deeply into her eyes. "Most especially, my heart."

Gloria lifted her eyes to meet him. Hannah watched as a sneer crossed over her face. "Oh, honey. If you believe that I would want you without my grandfather's money, you are dumber than I thought you were."

Frederick's face went stark white. His hands began shaking as he reached for hers. "Surely, you are joking?" he asked.

Gloria stood up from the couch. "Surely, you're an idiot." She turned and left the room, never once looking behind her.

Frederick slumped into his chair, his glasses sliding down his nose as he stared off in the distance in disbelief. Mazie sensed that her friend wasn't feeling his best and ran to jump on his lap, then began nuzzling his face. Despite his sadness, he was able to lift the corners of his mouth with a slight smile. "Thanks, Mazie," he whispered, closing his eyes to enjoy the only affection he would receive for a while.

Hannah and Pilar looked on, extending sympathetic glances toward the accountant.

"It can be tough for an accountant when things don't add up, despite calculating them neatly in your mind," Pilar said her deep brown eyes softening as she watched the miserable man.

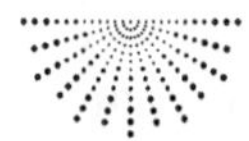

CHAPTER TEN

Several weeks later, Hannah and Colin were sitting at their special table in their favorite coffee shop - Jolt of Java. The fire crackled behind them, lending to the comfort of their afternoon. Mazie slept soundly in the dog bed by the fire, while the couple enjoyed sipping their steaming lattes.

Anita had noticed their arrival and kept eyeing them, waiting for the moment she could head over and catch up with her two friends. She had been playing phone tag with Hannah for the last couple of weeks and still hadn't heard the full story from her recent murder case.

Finally, there was a lull in the customer flow and

Anita was able to join them. Hannah watched as she hustled over, wide-eyed and anticipatory. The wind from her hurried entrance swept over Hannah and she smelled the freshly roasted beans on Anita's apron. "Tell me all about it!" Anita said, ripping a piece of her croissant off and tossing it to Mazie.

"I'm sure you've heard that Justin Blake has been arrested for the murder of Lucas Blake, his grandfather," Hannah said.

"Yes, I've been following along via the news. With each article I read, I can't help but wonder what the back story is. I've been dying to hear your side of things!" she said to Hannah.

Hannah grabbed Colin's hand. "As a matter of fact, Colin and I were at the Blakes' estate at a party the night he was murdered," she said.

Anita's eyes widened.

"Pilar, their former accountant caused quite a scene and had to be escorted out of the party, and we thought that was the extent of the excitement for the night, but we left for home and got a call later from Kate telling us that Lucas had been murdered."

Anita's hands clasped her heart as she leaned forward, waiting for more.

"His granddaughter, Gloria, had forged documents and faked a romantic interest in the new accountant, Frederick, to attempt to secure the family fortune; meanwhile, her bother, Justin, was the real killer, and we tricked him into inadvertently confessing by telling him about Frederick's special ink," she said.

Hannah wasn't sure if Anita fully understood the details, but she didn't seem to mind. Since tagging along with Hannah to solve a crime, she considered herself a junior detective and loved hearing each and every detail. "So, Justin is behind bars," Hannah said.

"Well, where did Gloria end up?" Anita asked. "It sounds like she wasn't completely innocent, forging documents that way."

"No, but there was no one to press charges against her. The police were more concerned with capturing a killer, as I'm sure you'd understand," Hannah said.

Colin jumped in at this point. "It sounds like Gloria left Blairstown pretty quickly after her brother's arrest," Colin said.

"And after breaking Frederick's heart," Hannah added. Hannah still had a soft spot for Frederick and couldn't believe how unlucky in love he had been with Gloria.

"Speaking of Frederick, I've tried to get in touch with him after Justin's arrest, but he fled pretty quickly as well," Colin said.

"If I hadn't watched Gloria break his heart with my own eyes, I'd wonder if maybe he skipped town with her," Hannah added. "I just hope he's doing okay."

Mazie's ears suddenly went back as if she heard something familiar. She stretched in her bed then stood on all four legs and began sniffing the air. Then without any warning, she darted to the front door of the coffee shop. Hannah, Colin, and Anita watched her sprint and stop abruptly at the feet of Jolt of Java's newest patron. Hannah's eyes followed his feet up to his face when she gasped in recognition. Standing up, she rushed over to greet him. "Frederick! We were just talking about you! How are you? Where have you been? Come, join us over here," she gushed.

A light blush filled Frederick's cheeks as he followed

Hannah to the table, scratching Mazie's back as he went.

Colin stood to greet his accountant, looking relieved, he commented, "Frederick, my man. You are looking excellent. Have you been working out, or have you gone somewhere sunny?"

Hannah had to agree, Frederick's complexion looked brighter, and his eyes had a tell-tale spark to them.

Frederick grinned, pushing his glasses up his nose, then he took a seat. "Well, funny you should say so, Colin, because I'm feeling excellent. Marriage can have that effect on a man!" he announced.

Hannah felt her blood turn ice cold. Had he really gone after Gloria, after everything she had done to him, the horrible way she had treated him? "Frederick, did you marry Gloria?" Hannah whispered, afraid to say the words too loud in case they were true. Mazie released a low growl at the mere mention of the woman's name.

Frederick's eyes opened with recognition, seeming to realize the implication of what he'd just said. "Oh! No! I did not marry Gloria!" he waved his hands in front of them as if to ward off the negativity of her name. "I met a woman after Gloria left me. She is beautiful, she is intelligent, and she is kind," he beamed.

Hannah felt a huge relief at his words, then looked past him to the door. "It must be an accountant conference - there is Pilar!" she said, waving at the woman to come over and join them.

Pilar saw them and her eyes lit up like fireworks. She all but ran over to greet them. Hannah was surprised at her enthusiasm, given that they didn't know one another incredibly well, but then she assumed it was because she'd freed her from being wrongfully imprisoned. Hannah stood to greet her in a warm hug. Pilar headed toward her but didn't stop at Hannah; instead, she ran right past her and launched herself into Frederick's arms.

Frederick held her tightly and kissed her cheek before releasing her. He grabbed her hand and faced the others at the table. "Pilar and I began talking in the wake of everything that happened. You can imagine that we had quite a bit to talk about," he lifted his brows and the listening group chuckled knowingly.

"As it turns out, we had more in common than just the Blake account," he said.

Pilar stood next to him, beaming. "We quickly found out that we are soulmates," she said. "We fell in love in short order and decided that neither one of us needed to be lonely anymore." She looked up to Frederick, and he bent to give her a quick kiss.

Colin clapped his hands. "This is such excellent news!" he said. "Frederick, I'm so happy for you. It seems as if you've really met your match."

Anita leaned her cheek on her hands. "Congrats, you two."

Hannah stood to give hugs to Frederick and Pilar. "I am so glad that something good came out of the entire situation," she said. "You two couldn't be a more perfect match. I'm so thrilled for you both!"

"Thank you so much, Hannah," Pilar said. "Your name has come up often between us. We wouldn't be together if it weren't for you and Mazie pointing us in the right direction. I'm so glad I trusted you when you found me at that dingy, old motel!" she said.

Mazie barked happily and wagged her tail, seeming to understand her part in the happily ever after of Pilar and Frederick. The group laughed at the beagle's human-like tendencies, once again.

Hannah couldn't help but admire the beaming couple. She'd hoped for this exact happiness for Frederick when she first met him but couldn't have imagined the way it came to be. She reached to hold Colin's hand and squeezed it tight. Colin leaned to give her a kiss on the cheek.

"Please, will you both sit and join us for a celebratory cup of coffee? We'd love to toast to your future!" Hannah said.

Pilar looked at Frederick who nodded. "That would be fantastic, thank you for the offer."

"Oh!" Anita said. "I may just have some champagne in the back. Oscar and I keep some chilled for special occasions. Why don't I go grab it and make it a proper celebration?" she asked.

Frederick and Pilar exchanged a glance, and Pilar burst into laughter. Frederick looked at the group sheepishly. "To be honest, I haven't touched any alcohol since the party at the Blake house," he said.

Pilar rubbed his arm affectionately as he continued. "I think it's safe to say that a black coffee is the best drink for me to celebrate anything important."

Hannah burst into laughter, remembering his antics at the party. Now that they had captured the killer, it felt okay to laugh about it. "Great point, Frederick. We want to be sure you remember the celebration this time," she joked.

Frederick smiled good-naturedly and Oscar came over with a tray of fresh drinks for everyone. "I hear we are celebrating something?" he said, handing a cup to each person.

"To a lifetime of happiness for Frederick and Pilar," Colin said, raising a glass.

Their mugs met in the air. "To Frederick and Pilar!" the rest of them repeated, and they all sipped their drinks.

The Bakers and Bulldogs Mysteries Collection – Preview

Grab this 20 book box set for FREE with Kindle Unlimited here

Ding. Melody stretched the dough a little further; holding her breath as she expertly pulled it just enough to ensure a perfectly thin, translucent layer. The bell pinged again, and Melody glanced around for Kerry.

"Hey, Ker—where are you?" she called, failing to detect her assistant's presence. Melody shook her head, wiped her hands on her apron, exited the kitchen and hurried into the shop. There stood her best customer, Alvin Hennessy, the small town's local sheriff, his kind brown eyes lighting up as Melody came into his view. He hastily removed his hat, cleared his throat and smiled sheepishly down at her.

"Oh, hey there, Mel. Sorry to stop in again today, but I forgot I needed a cake for Ma's hen party tonight." Alvin shuffled his feet shyly, his cheeks reddening.

Melody sighed. She was grateful for his business, but suspected he purposely cut his order in two so he had an excuse to drop by twice today. She would have preferred efficiency, but good manners and a genuine fondness for the sheriff prevented her from showing any exasperation. She should be flattered by his attention—she knew, but she really wasn't interested in a romantic relationship at this point in her life. Not that he wasn't handsome, in his own way, but he was just not her type, she supposed, even if she *were* in the market for a romantic relationship. She took a quick moment to evaluate his appearance. He possessed the long, lean lines of a thoroughbred, but somehow wasn't able to project his inherent attractiveness, even in uniform. Perhaps it was his constant grinning. It made him appear a little strange, no, that wasn't really it; it was more his inability to realize his own appeal, a slight insecurity, an awkwardness. She mentally shook herself and focused on the business at hand.

"Not a problem, Al. Always good to see you!" she said, forcing a smile.

She felt a pang of guilt at her fib, but knew she probably made his day with her comment. In spite of her uncanny ability to notice and discern the overt as well as hidden attributes of others, Melody possessed a baffling blindness to her own qualities. She could have easily graced the pages of any magazine, even in jeans and her trademark logoed tee. An Irish beauty, Melody was blessed with more than her fair share of pluses: glossy auburn, shoulder-length tresses (albeit piled on her head and anchored with a hairnet), an angelic face, and statuesque curves to rival any pin-up girl. She had many secret (and not so secret) male admirers in town, but even though she was consistently friendly and courteous, she possessed an intimidating blend of self-assurance, the formerly discussed unawareness of her beauty, and a steadfast personal rule against flirting.

"What kind of cake did you have in mind? We have a cream cheese-filled red velvet and an orange-hickory nut on hand. Kerry made them yesterday, and they're still fresh."

As if summoned by her name, Kerry rushed in, flinging out hyper apologies as she whipped on an apron over her uniform of sparkly blue jeans and the shop's logo-emblazoned t-shirt.

"Where were you?" Melody asked.

"I forgot my phone in my car and wanted to make sure Aunt Rita didn't call with her family reunion order. I told her to call the shop rather than my cell, but she never remembers the number and can't be bothered to look it up. Good thing I checked; as she did leave me a voicemail with what she wants, and she's hoping to get everything tomorrow afternoon, even though the reunion doesn't start until Friday evening!" Kerry's words tumbled over each other as her hands gestured wildly. Melody wondered how Kerry was able to breathe while talking at such a rate.

"I see you've gone over your quota of caffeine today," Melody teased, noting Kerry's messy blond bun slipping out of the hair net stretched crookedly over her head and the slight sheen of sweat on her brow.

Kerry, plump and pretty, was engaged to Port Warren High's beloved football coach, George Stanley, who adored her. In Kerry's mind, this gave her free reign to play matchmaker with all her unfortunately single friends and acquaintances, especially her beautiful boss.

"Yeah, might have overdone the go-juice just a tad." Kerry chuckled, tucking her stray blond strands back into the net. Kerry then turned her attention to their visitor. "Hey, Al, you forget something? Weren't you in earlier?"

Alvin blushed and nodded, looking down at his shoes and rubbing his close-cropped brown hair.

Kerry smiled wickedly at his obvious discomfiture. "I'm beginning to think this is your new office!"

Melody gave her a quick, pursed lip glare, knowing it would only encourage her would-be marriage broker to continue to tease poor Alvin.

"Yep, completely forgot about Ma's card deal tonight; she wanted me to pick up a cake; whatcha got in stock?" Alvin asked trying to recover himself.

As the sheriff switched his embarrassed attention to

his torturer, Melody took the opportunity to slip quietly back into the kitchen to finish the croissants, leaving Kerry to fill Alvin's order. She concentrated, cutting and folding thin strips into perfect crescents.

"That guy's got it bad!" Kerry announced as she sailed into the kitchen, automatically beelining it for the coffee machine.

"No! You're cut off!" Melody was quick to see her assistant's intention and she grabbed Kerry's sleeve with a floury hand, "No more coffee for you!"

Kerry sheepishly set the pot back down and crossed her arms. She eyed the tray of bakery rejects that failed Melody's perfectionistic eye, sighed, and helped herself to a broken cookie. Nibbling, she glared at Melody.

"You've got it bad," Melody insisted. "You're torturing that poor man, and you know it! What did he end up buying?"

"Don't try and change the subject! That dog is one whipped puppy. If he really forgot that cake this morning, I'm a one-eyed frog. His mom has bridge every Wednesday night, tonight is no exception!"

Kerry exclaimed while munching through a second cookie reject.

Melody shrugged, not wanting to encourage that line of thinking. She'd known for a while that Alvin had a thing for her. She tried her best to ignore it and avoid him as much as possible. With her busy schedule, she just wasn't ready for anything serious, even if it was with someone like Alvin. Or was it really about her schedule? Whatever, she was just not into a relationship at the moment. She had to admit, he was a good guy. And he would probably treat her right if she ever gave him a chance. But it was just too soon.

"He's either going to have to man up and ask you out or go broke buying donuts and cakes! For a lawman, he ain't very brave!" Kerry added.

Melody let her rattle on, hoping Kerry would run out of words on the subject, though that seemed unlikely.

Kerry propped her chin on her left palm looking all dreamy. "I think he's cute, though, don't you? A little on the puppy dog side, but still pretty manly when he's not tripping over his tongue when you're around."

Melody sighed, rolled her eyes, and kept silent. It was her weapon of choice and it worked well with Kerry, whose main hobby was verbalizing, combined with taking off on frequent, caffeine-infused rabbit trails. So, Kerry prattled on while Mel took a moment to mull over the situation.

In truth, she almost wished she reciprocated Alvin's apparent feelings. She dreaded the day she would really have to reject such a nice guy. She blew out a breath of frustration, hoping against hope that he would never find the courage to approach her romantically because in that way she could avoid the whole ordeal. If he did ever find the courage to ask her out, she would just have to find a nice way to turn him down. Maybe she should start thinking about how she could get out of it without hurting his feelings.

Her thoughts, generally practical, quickly switched over to Aunt Rita's reunion and she broke into Kerry's monologue.

"Which cake did the sheriff end up buying? And what does Aunt Rita need by Friday?" Melody asked and Kerry cooperated with the subject change, her talking talent showcased by her ability to jump off and on any topic train.

"He decided on the red velvet. Auntie said she needs three cakes: one devil's food, one pineapple upside down, and one hummingbird. I think I should call her and steer her away from the hummingbird, as it's too similar to the pineapple upside-down—don't you think? Maybe a pecan Texas sheet instead? Add a little variety? Also, she wants two-dozen each of chocolate chip, shortbread and peanut butter cookies, an apple strudel and six dozen dinner rolls. I think I better tell her to freeze everything when she gets it tomorrow since she's not serving most of it until Saturday and Sunday, and I wouldn't think she'd like them anything but fresh. Really, she should get everything from us Friday afternoon; we could have it done by two, don't you think? Maybe I should call her? Maybe not, as she never changes her mind once she makes a plan; maybe you should call her? She'd probably listen to you better than me. But maybe freezing them would be good enough and then we wouldn't be as stressed on Saturday, as we have that wedding cake to deliver and set up, and Jeannette isn't somebody we want to disappoint with shoddy work..." Kerry continued to ponder the quandary of her aunt's order while she bustled about wiping counters, putting away clean tools from the dish drainer, and checking—and double-checking—the stores of supplies.

Just then the bell dinged, heralding another customer, and Kerry whisked out of the kitchen.

Melody opened the oven and placed the croissant trays inside, setting the timer as she finished. She could hear Kerry's voice, presumably talking to a customer, and while tempted to start on tomorrow's orders, she knew she should make an appearance in the shop as some of her customers took it very personally when she was too busy to greet them.

Kerry's Aunt Rita stood at the counter, her lips pursed as she listened to her niece's flood of advice. Rita held up her hand, finally getting Kerry to slow her word flow. Aunt Rita had a closet full of old-fashioned, 50's style dresses that belted at the waist, everything from floral, to stripes and plaids, to plain. She only ever wore dark brown, laced up walking shoes, white gloves, and netted hats whenever she ventured outside her house. Inside, she wore button-up housedresses, ones she deemed suitable for the constant cleaning she inflicted on her house. Dust was terrified to land anywhere in her vicinity.

"I need everything by tomorrow afternoon, Kerry Ann, is that going to be a problem?" Just as Kerry opened her mouth to answer, Rita caught sight of Melody.

"Thank God you're here! My niece seems to think I don't know my own mind, and I need her to understand that I need everything tomorrow afternoon. I will be extremely busy with other reunion tasks... of course, I have to do everything myself, the rest of the family cannot be trusted... so I need the desserts squared away tomorrow. Is that too difficult?" Rita glared at Melody belligerently.

"Oh no, Rita, tomorrow afternoon is perfect! We don't have another big order besides yours due until Friday afternoon, so it will work out just fine, and your choices show nice forethought and variety," Melody assured her.

"Hmph. Kerry Ann here seems to think I don't have enough variety in the cake department. I keep trying to explain that Cousin Harold loves the pineapple upside down and my sister must have hummingbird.

There is no room for substitutes. Now, I need to know if those choices are going to be a problem? I don't want to take my business elsewhere, but my friend Alice's cousin bakes and sells cakes out of her kitchen, so I do have other options," Rita continued to scowl pugnaciously at her niece while she directed her question to Melody.

"No, we can certainly bake all your choices," Melody replied calmly. "All your selections are just fine, and there is no finer cake baker than your niece here!"

Mollified, Kerry let go of her need to adjust Aunt Rita's cake menu, and smiled at her employer, "Awww shucks, boss-lady! You're the best!"

"Hmph," Rita grunted, clutching her giant purse more firmly to her chest, as if perhaps Melody and Kerry weren't to be trusted; she then adjusted her old-fashioned hat and exited with, "Okay then. I'll expect your delivery tomorrow afternoon, but no earlier than two pm, as I'll need an afternoon rest with all this working myself to death. And for what? Some ungrateful relatives who don't mind reaping the benefits of all my back-breaking labor!"

Kerry groaned, shaking her head. As soon as her aunt

was out of earshot, she commented, "Oh my God, Aunt Rita is something else, isn't she? No wonder Uncle Leroy left this earth… her sunny disposition probably poisoned him to death!"

Melody smiled, suspecting Kerry probably inherited her aunt's opinionated personality, and ability to talk at lightspeed. Though Kerry was liberally tempered with cheerfulness, Rita lacked pretty much any positive modifying trait.

Grab The Bakers and Bulldog Mysteries Collection now

If you enjoyed this book, Rosie and Agatha would appreciate it if you left a review on Amazon or Goodreads